Dinosaur School

DINOSAUR HOLIDAYS

Joyce Jeffries

Please visit our website, www.garethstevens.com. For a free color catalog of all our high-quality books, call toll free 1-800-542-2595 or fax 1-877-542-2596.

Library of Congress Cataloging-in-Publication Data

Jeffries, Joyce.
Dinosaur holidays / by Joyce Jeffries.
   p. cm. — (Dinosaur school)
Includes index.
ISBN 978-1-4824-0737-2 (pbk.)
ISBN 978-1-4824-0761-7 (6-pack)
ISBN 978-1-4824-0738-9 (library binding)
1. Holidays — Juvenile literature. 2. Dinosaurs — Juvenile literature. I. Jeffries, Joyce. II. Title.
GT3933.J44 2015
394.26—d23

First Edition

Published in 2015 by
Gareth Stevens Publishing
111 East 14th Street, Suite 349
New York, NY 10003

Designer: Andrea Davison-Bartolotta
Editor: Ryan Nagelhout

All illustrations by Contentra Technologies

CPSIA compliance information: Batch #CS15GS: For further information contact Gareth Stevens, New York, New York at 1-800-542-2595.

DINOSAUR HOLIDAYS

By Joyce Jeffries

Gareth Stevens
PUBLISHING

Dinosaurs love the holidays.

We love to celebrate.

I love Earth Day!

6

I plant a tree.

I clean up litter.

I plant a garden!

9

I love the Fourth of July!

I put out our flag.

I go to a parade.

I see fireworks.

I love Halloween!

I go pick pumpkins.

I wear a costume.

I get lots of candy!

I love Thanksgiving!

I eat a big dinner!

I eat pumpkin pie.

I play football with friends.

I love Valentine's Day!

I give valentines to
my friends!

Dinosaur Holidays